# SELECTED MAGNIFICATS

# RECENT RESEARCHES IN THE MUSIC OF THE BAROQUE ERA

*Robert L. Marshall, general editor*

---

A-R Editions, Inc., publishes six quarterly series—

*Recent Researches in the Music of the Middle Ages and Early Renaissance,*
Margaret Bent, general editor;

*Recent Researches in the Music of the Renaissance,*
James Haar and Howard Mayer Brown, general editors;

*Recent Researches in the Music of the Baroque Era,*
Robert L. Marshall, general editor;

*Recent Researches in the Music of the Classical Era,*
Eugene K. Wolf, general editor;

*Recent Researches in the Music of the Nineteenth and Early Twentieth Centuries,*
Jerald C. Graue, general editor;

*Recent Researches in American Music,*
H. Wiley Hitchcock, general editor—

which make public music that is being brought to light
in the course of current musicological research.

Each volume in the *Recent Researches* is devoted
to works by a single composer or to a single genre of composition,
chosen because of its potential interest to scholars and performers,
and prepared for publication according to the standards that govern
the making of all reliable historical editions.

Subscribers to this series, as well as patrons of subscribing institutions,
are invited to apply for information about the "Copyright-Sharing Policy"
of A-R Editions, Inc., under which the contents of this volume
may be reproduced free of charge for study or performance.

Correspondence should be addressed:

A-R EDITIONS, INC.
315 West Gorham Street
Madison, Wisconsin 53703

RECENT RESEARCHES IN THE MUSIC OF THE BAROQUE ERA • VOLUME XXXV

Johann Stadlmayr

# SELECTED MAGNIFICATS

Edited by Hilde Junkermann
with Basso Continuo Realizations and Commentary
by Marilyn Barnes-Ostrander

A-R EDITIONS, INC. • MADISON

Copyright © 1980, A-R Editions, Inc.

ISSN 0484-0828

ISBN 0-89579-132-3

Library of Congress Cataloging in Publication Data:
Stadlmayr, Johann, 1560 (ca.)-1648.
    Selected Magnificats.

    (Recent researches in the music of the baroque era ; v.
35 ISSN 0484-0828)
    Includes bibliographical references.
    CONTENTS: Magnificat super Spuntavan già, à 5, 1603,
no. 1 (SSATB)—Magnificat super D'un si bel fuoco, à 6,
1603, no. 3 (SSATTB)—Magnificat, à 7, 1603, no. 7
(SSAATTB)—[etc.]
    1. Part-songs, Sacred.   2. Choruses, Sacred (Mixed
voices)   3. Magnificat (Music)   I. Junkermann, Hilde.
II. Barnes-Ostrander, Marilyn.   III. Title:
Magnificats.   IV. Series.
M2.R238.R238   vol. 35   [M3.1]   [M2079.L6]   780'.903'3s
ISBN 0-89579-132-3                      [783.6'75]   80-24341

# Contents

# Preface

## The Composer

Johann Stadlmayr was one of the leading figures among the early seventeenth-century masters who composed for the Roman Church service as it was celebrated in South Germany and Austria.[1] However, little is known about his early years, and to date no records of his birth or baptism have been found. In an Innsbruck court document of 1619, Stadlmayr is described as "a rather young and lively man." That description and the date of 1596 for his first publication[2] indicate that Stadlmayr may have been born sometime around the year 1575. The title page and dedication of Stadlmayr's Magnificat settings published in 1603[3] establish that he came from Freising (Bavaria), which was then the residence of prince-bishops who enjoyed and supported a distinguished musical life. At the time of this 1603 publication, Stadlmayr was employed by Prince Bishop Wolf Dietrich von Raitenau in Salzburg. The composer held the post of Salzburg *Hofkapellmeister* from 1604 until 1607, when he was appointed to the same office at the Innsbruck court of the Habsburg Archduke Maximilian II of Tyrol. Once established in Innsbruck, Stadlmayr remained there until his death in 1648, though other positions were offered to him during his later years.

Hard times for Stadlmayr came in 1619 under Maximilian's successor, Archduke Leopold V, who also served as Bishop of Strassburg and thus did not use Innsbruck as his chief residence. The Innsbruck chapel was largely disbanded, and Stadlmayr's income was reduced to a meager pension. Several of the composer's petitions for renewed professional employment remained unheeded, so that Stadlmayr was forced to supplement his income by working as government meat inspector for Innsbruck. Finally in 1624, having asked for permission to apply for a post in Vienna, he was reappointed as Innsbruck *Hofkapellmeister* with a commensurate salary. Two years later Archduke Leopold married Claudia de' Medici, known for her excellent education and cultivated taste. Claudia gave solid support to *Kapellmeister* Stadlmayr—including financial assistance for the publication of some of his works—even during the difficult times that followed her husband's death in 1632. Under her patronage, the Innsbruck *Hofkapelle* directed by Stadlmayr attained its greatest brilliance.

At the Innsbruck court, located near the strategic Brenner Pass, Stadlmayr was exposed to the international cultural exchange so characteristic of the Habsburg dynasty. Indeed, the Habsburgs' court had been flourishing long before Stadlmayr came to Innsbruck. Visual testimony to Habsburg power and patronage of the arts is admired to this day. Such testimony includes the grand memorial to Emperor Maximilian I in the nave of the *Hofkirche*, where twenty-eight bronze statues of illustrious men and women belonging to the Habsburg lineage and of heroes from medieval Christianity and the age of chivalry surround the cenotaph of the emperor. Another famous Habsburg memorial in the *Hofkirche* is the Silver Chapel (completed in 1587), burial place of Archduke Ferdinand II of Tyrol and his morganatic first wife, Philippine Welser of the Augsburg merchant dynasty. Innsbruck's musical and artistic life flourished with particular splendor under the enlightened rule of this prince (from 1565 to 1596), bolstered, no doubt, by Welser money. During the last ten years of this period, the renowned Netherlander Jacob Regnart (ca. 1530 to ca. 1600) was one of Stadlmayr's predecessors as *Hofkapellmeister*. Detailed inventories dating from before and during Stadlmayr's time document a rich store of musical instruments and a large collection of music manuscripts and prints in sacred and secular genres available for worship services and entertainments.

## The Music

Stadlmayr's sacred works were praised beyond the Innsbruck of his day.[4] They include collections of Masses, Magnificat settings, Introits, antiphons, Vesper Psalms, and hymns. An edition of some of Stadlmayr's hymn settings is, to date, the only modern publication of his works.[5] However, a number of his compositions appear in seventeenth-century anthologies used from Italy to the Low Countries, as well as in widely dispersed keyboard intabulations. Moreover, some of Stadlmayr's works continued to be performed in the eighteenth century. Their well-deserved renown resulted from Stadlmayr's solid musical craftsmanship and his ability to create varied works of art from modest material with relatively simple means.

His compositional style was influenced both by liturgical traditions and by seventeenth-century innovations. These influences are apparent in the thirty-eight extant Magnificat settings. The eight chosen for this edition exemplify these stylistic traits.

Stadlmayr prints issued in 1603, 1614, and 1618 are devoted exclusively to Magnificat settings. Another publication, issued in 1608, contains eight Magnificats as well as some other liturgical works of his. The 1618 print is the last contemporary edition to be comprised solely of Stadlmayr Magnificats. Because of the extensive performance forces required, none of the works from this print are included in the present edition. Entitled *Cantici Mariani . . .*, this print was issued by Daniel Agricola in Innsbruck.[6] The seven works included are cast in the polychoral Venetian style. Four of them are parody compositions, and three others are based on Canticle Tones.

Stadlmayr's remaining extant Magnificat settings appeared in two collections of his Vesper Psalms, published in 1640 and 1641 by Michael Wagner in Innsbruck.[7] Each collection includes two Magnificat settings, one rather simple and the other more elaborate, as was customary for such publications. The 1640 collection now lacks what was probably a second tenor partbook. Because the 1641 print is a source for a Magnificat setting included in the present edition, it will be discussed below in the section on sources.

Stadlmayr's Magnificats exemplify the mixture of styles found in European music of the early seventeenth century. The clear articulation of the text required by the Council of Trent is achieved by the use of short phrases that carry a generally syllabic declamation governed by the speech inflection of the Latin words. In the manner of sixteenth-century motets, each text phrase of Stadlmayr's Magnificats generates its own musical motif, especially its rhythmic pattern, so that text repetitions, either in imitation or in sequence, produce musical similarities, too. The composer gave special text passages or words expressive emphasis by drawing on the then widely shared vocabulary of musical *figurae*.[8]

His earlier Magnificat settings have the texture of sixteenth-century polyphony; moreover, this polyphony is often combined in these works with sections in polychoral Venetian style. Another sixteenth-century tradition preserved in Stadlmayr's settings is the use of the eight Magnificat-Canticle chants, or Tones[9] (sometimes for *cantus firmi* set in long notes, and sometimes as bases for melodies within the settings). Sixteen of Stadlmayr's Magnificat settings have titles relating them to one of the eight Canticle Tones; melodic references to Canticle Tones are apparent in

two additional settings, although their titles do not name the Tones. Nineteen other Stadlmayr Magnificats make use of yet another important compositional device, namely, parody technique. Parody technique involves the incorporation of the harmonic, melodic, and rhythmic characteristics of a pre-existent composition (the model) into a new work; this differs from techniques that incorporate only a pre-existent melody. Only one of the thirty-eight extant Magnificat settings lacks an obvious reference to a pre-existing composition or chant formula. (See the discussion of 1603, No. 7, below.)

The ancient tradition of antiphonal psalmody, also used for the Magnificat-Canticles, where two groups sing successive verses in alternation, is reflected in the twenty-eight of Stadlmayr's Magnificats where only the even-numbered verses are set by the composer; the odd-numbered verses are to be sung to the appropriate chant formulae. Even in the remaining ten Stadlmayr Magnificats, where the entire text is set, a clear differentiation in style or texture is made between odd- and even-numbered verses. Moreover, the binary musical forms of many individual verses reflect the two-part verbal structure of each verse of the Magnificat text.

A shift to the new, seventeenth-century, style is acknowledged in the works from the year 1614 and after by the use of added *basso ad organum* parts (see the Appendix for a commentary on the *basso continuo* realizations, provided for the last three Magnificats in the present edition); actually, these parts merely double the lowest vocal part in the manner of a *basso seguente*. In addition, several Magnificat settings from the later period include solo parts in various combinations of voices; some of these vocal solos are accompanied by two treble instruments (violins or *cornetti*) deployed in imitative, often florid concertato fashion in contrast to chordal sections of the tutti groups. The later works emerge from modality into the major/minor divisions of modern tonality as manifested in the increasing number of what we would now call dominant/tonic cadences.

## The Magnificats and their Sources

### The Print of 1603

The first four Magnificat settings in the present edition were originally issued in a collection (where they were numbered 1, 3, 7, and 9) of ten Stadlmayr Magnificats brought out in 1603 by the Munich printers Adam Berg and Heinrich Nicolaus under the title *Sacrum Beatissimae Virginis Mariae Canticum 5.6.7.8.v.*; Stadlmayr dedicated the publication to his employer, Salzburg's Archbishop-Prince Wolf Dietrich von Raitenau. In all but the last work (No. 10) of this 1603 collection, only the even-numbered verses of the text are set polyphonically; the odd-numbered verses are to be sung according to the Canticle formula appropriate to the mode of the composed verses.[10]

Six of the Magnificats in this print are parody compositions on Italian madrigals; one is modeled after a Latin motet as yet unidentified (No. 5, "Benedictus Deus"). Where both the parody composition and the model from which it is derived are known, their relationship to one another is unmistakable. Such derivation is especially evident at the very beginning of each parody composition, and sometimes also at the beginnings of later sections. Thus Stadlmayr acknowledged the contribution made by the model both by citing its title (e.g., *Magnificat super Spuntavan già*) and by quoting it literally—reproducing notation, texture, melody, rhythm, and harmony—at these especially exposed phrases. Moreover, in each case the style of the model directly influenced the style of the entire parody Magnificat.

The collection of 1603 is arranged according to the number of parts in each Magnificat, beginning with works for five parts and ending with those for eight. In accord with traditional practice, Stadlmayr reduced the number of voices for at least one of the verses (usually the eighth) in each Magnificat setting of the 1603 collection.

## 1603, No. 1, Magnificat super Spuntavan già à 5

The collection of 1603 opens with a work based on one of Marenzio's best-known madrigals for five voices, *Spuntavan già*,[11] a light-hearted piece describing the bustling of awakening nature. Stadlmayr used the *chiavette* (a system of writing vocal music with the clefs moved from their normal position)[12] of the model for his five-voice Magnificat setting. But he changed the time signature from the *misura cromatica* (indicated by C in the madrigal) to the signature ₵, based on the breve as unit, adhering to the common practice of using this older form for sacred music. After the beginning of the Magnificat setting, which closely resembles the madrigal, the musical material of the model is taken apart, extended, and reworked in a number of ways, incorporating paraphrase and variation. Stadlmayr, apparently thoroughly familiar with the principles of musical rhetoric, took great care to select the most appropriate musical phrases from the madrigal model for the proper inflection and expressiveness of specific phrases in the Magnificat text. (The plainsong formula to be used for performance of the odd-numbered verses is Magnificat Tone 8, beginning and ending on g.)

## 1603, No. 3, Magnificat super D'un si bel fuoco à 6

Stadlmayr based this Magnificat on an attractive five-voice madrigal by Giaches de Wert.[13] This setting is especially interesting because Stadlmayr also used the plainsong formula of the Magnificat Canticle (Tone 1) in the composition, thus giving this setting the stamp of the Church. The *cantus firmus* is carried in

long note values by the Quinta Vox throughout the setting. Moreover, for each composed verse, this Canticle melody is interwoven in quite an individual manner with the other five voices, all based on the musical fabric of the madrigal.

## 1603, No. 7, Magnificat à 7

The absence of a subtitle for the seventh Magnificat in the source collection indicates a departure from the parody method used in the preceding works of the 1603 print. Instead, strict contrapuntal procedures are emphasized: two inner parts, the Altus and Septima Vox, form six different canons in unison for the six polyphonically set verses (verses 2, 4, 6, 8, 10, and 12). Only the four highest voices participate in the relatively brief tenth verse, "Sicut locutus est." Here the reduction in the number of parts is compensated for by the added complexity in the polyphonic texture resulting from a double canon; one canon is between the Discantus and Quinta Vox, the other canon, on a different melody, is between the Altus and Septima Vox. (The plainsong formula to be used for performance of the odd-numbered verses is Tone 8.)

## 1603, No. 9, Magnificat [Quarti Toni] à 8

This Magnificat setting is marked by the combination of three compositional procedures. Two of these concern the texture, which includes imitative polyphony as well as polychoral treatment in various sections of this eight-part (SS AA TT BB, in modern terminology) Magnificat. Examples of imitative polyphony occur at the beginning of Verses 2, 8, and 12. Although Stadlmayr did not divide the eight voice lines into two distinct choirs, he worked with various groupings of four voices set against the remaining four. Examples of such polychoral treatment are found in Verse 4, mm. 1-11, and in Verse 10, mm. 1-4 and mm. 19-23. The third compositional procedure used here concerns the derivation of a few melodic phrases from plainsong. The long notes in the incipit of the Sexta Vox provide a clue, as does the subtitle given the work in the concordant Kremsmünster Choirbook L 1,[14] ". . . super quartum tonum." This subtitle refers to an early version of the Fourth Magnificat Tone. Not in the *Liber Usualis*, but found in modern editions of the *Antiphonale monasticum*,[15] this early version is to be used here as an alternating plainsong formula for performance of the odd-numbered Magnificat verses:

### The Print of 1608

The fifth work in the present edition, the *Magnificat Primi Toni*, first appeared in a set of eight Magnificats published with some other liturgical works in 1608 under the title *Magnificat quatuor vocum super octo tonos, quibus accesserunt Litaniae, Antiphonae Mariales octo vocum.*[16] As indicated on the title page, Stadlmayr was by this time in the service of Archduke Maximilian II of Austria, then governor of Tyrol. Only three of the partbooks (Cantus, Altus, and Bassus) from this publication are extant.[17] However, these Magnificats are complete in the Choirbook Mus. Mss. 88 of the Bavarian State Library in Munich. Thus, the Tenor part in the present edition has been supplied from this manuscript, while all other parts are taken from the print of 1608 for the *Magnificat Primi Toni.* The Choirbook Mus. Mss. 88 must predate the 1608 print, since its title page refers to Stadlmayr's Salzburg employment, which preceded his position with Archduke Maximilian in Innsbruck. Although the manuscript is undated, an earlier date for the composition of the works of Mus. Mss. 88 may be established because the *Magnificat Quinti Toni* of Mus. Mss. 88 also opens the Kremsmünster Choirbook *L 5,* listed in the monastery's inventory of 1600.[18]

The composer dedicated the publication of 1608 to a very specific image of the Virgin, the patroness of the basilica in Öttingen, Bavaria (now Altötting). The Holy Chapel there with its famous Madonna had long been a place of pilgrimage for Roman Catholics from Central Europe.[19] Moreover, this small chapel was especially suited to performance of works of modest dimensions, such as those in the 1608 print, and we may assume that the composer intended these works for services in this chapel.

Stadlmayr followed the common Renaissance practice of setting each of the Magnificats in this 1608 publication to one of the eight plainsong Canticle Tones, with odd-numbered verses assigned to chant, and even-numbered verses set in four-part polyphony. The Canticle Tones, from which the melodic motives are drawn, are still in use today.[20] Frequently all elements of the Canticle formula, *initium, mediatio, finalis,* and *tuba* (reciting tone) appear in each polyphonic verse of these eight settings, usually to the same text sections as in the monophonic chant. Melodic fragments of the Canticle Tone may be found in any of the four voice-parts, successively or simultaneously.

The text treatment in these Magnificats is largely syllabic; word or phrase repetitions are minimal, so that the settings are quite short. Chordal and imitative textures are found in about equal proportions.

## 1608, No. 1, MAGNIFICAT PRIMI TONI

For this Magnificat, the Canticle Tone 1 is transposed to g. Even within this modest framework Stadlmayr achieved variety: for instance, no two of the even-numbered polyphonic verses, brief though they are, follow the same pattern of text repetition or arrangement of textures; moreover, the verse beginnings show harmonic diversity, though the chant pattern is fundamental to all. The plainsong formula to be used for performance of the odd-numbered verses is Magnificat Tone 1, here transposed to accommodate this Magnificat setting:

### The Print of 1614

Stadlmayr's next Magnificat collection was published in 1614 by D. Agricola in Innsbruck under the title *Super Magnae Matris Divino Carmine. Magnificat. Symphoniae variae . . . 8.12 v. cum duplici basso organicorum.* It contains nine Magnificats. At this time, Stadlmayr, *Kapellmeister* for Archduke Maximilian in Innsbruck, dedicated these works to Anna Juliana, the revered widow of Maximilian's predecessor, Archduke Ferdinand II. This dedication of Magnificat settings was especially appropriate because the former Archduchess had entered the mendicant order of the Servites (Servants of Mary), which stands under special protection of the Blessed Virgin. Anna Juliana, known for her cultivated taste in music, continued her support of the arts even after taking the veil, thus greatly benefitting the quality of music-making at the convent chapel.

Eight of the nine Magnificats in this collection are for double chorus of four voices each; the last one is for twelve parts in triple chorus. The third and the eighth settings from the 1614 collection are included in the present edition.

This is the first Magnificat publication in Stadlmayr's output to take into account the new fashion of a written-out instrumental bass. However, in all but 1614, No. 3 (see below), the organ parts merely double the vocal basses of the double or triple choruses in the manner of a *basso seguente.* In the organ partbook the two, or three, bass lines are printed in score, as first observed by Otto Kinkeldey.[21]

The Magnificat titles in the 1614 print indicate that some of these works are parody compositions on secular and sacred models, while others are based on Canticle Tone 1. The first seven Magnificats of the 1614 print have composed settings for only the even-numbered verses; the eighth and ninth Magnificats are settings for all twelve verses of the entire text.

### 1614, No. 3, MAGNIFICAT LAUDANS EXULTANS à 8

This work is based on an eight-part motet, *Laudans exultet,* by Giovanni Croce (ca. 1557-1609), found in the third volume of the anthology *Promptuarii musici . . .,* edited by Abraham Schadeus and issued by Paul Ledertz in Strassburg in 1613.[22] The motet, honoring the Virgin, displays Croce's effective use of double chorus techniques as well as his careful attention to the Latin accentuation and meaning of the text. According to the fashion of the time, the works assembled by Schadeus for his anthology had been provided with an additional instrumental bass part, supplied by Caspar Vincentius.

In devising his Magnificat setting, Stadlmayr kept both the division of eight voices into two equal choirs and the *chiavette* combination of Croce's motet, but he gave each choir its own instrumental *basso seguente*, notated a fourth lower than the vocal basses.[23] Although he limited himself to only a few of the model's thematic ideas, Stadlmayr incorporated some of them almost literally into his Magnificat setting; he used other statements from Croce's motet as material for variation, and Croce's technique of expansion through repetition is evident in Stadlmayr's Magnificat as well.

In the Magnificat, the first section of the fourth verse, "Quia fecit . . . ," is set in triple meter. The most reliable clue to a correct transcription is the barring of the organ parts into regular breve units, entirely consistent for the duple meter sections, whereas the application of mensural signs is inconsistent throughout the volume in the very manner Praetorius criticized in his contemporaries.[24] (The plainsong formula to be used for performance of the odd-numbered verses is Magnificat Tone 6, beginning and ending on f.)

### 1614, No. 8, Magnificat super Primum Tonum à 8

This work differs in important ways from those preceding it in the present edition. The *Magnificat super Primum Tonum* is a setting of the complete Magnificat text, including the first word, "Magnificat." However, the *alternatim* idea, traditional in Magnificat composition, is maintained in this work by means of the differing textures in successive sections. The odd-numbered verses in the new concerted style, featuring solo voices accompanied by an independent *basso continuo*, contrast with the even-numbered ones, which are set in very simple double-chorus style with a great deal of doubling in some of the eight-part passages. Thematic unity is achieved by frequent melodic references to Canticle Tone 1, mentioned in the title of this work. The organ score in the *Bassus duplex pro organo* partbook provides a separate *continuo* line for each choir. In the odd-numbered verses Stadlmayr featured each of the four solo voices in turn, especially the Cantus, as the principal bearer of the canticle motives. The composer also combined solo voices into duets and expressed the climax of the Gloria section by using all four solo voices. Melismatic passages are especially notable in the Tenor of the seventh verse, "Deposuit. . . ."

### The Print of 1641

The organization of the 1641 collection, published by Michael Wagner in Innsbruck, shows what an eminently practical man Stadlmayr must have been. The publication is comprised of Vesper Psalms and two Magnificats, and the title, *Psalmi integri a 4 v. concertantibus, 4 aliis ad libitum . . .* , indicates that the works were conceived in such a way that they make complete musical sense when performed with either the first chorus alone or with both choruses. The four partbooks of the second chorus are marked "*Ripieni.*" The treble instruments, *cornetti* or violins, and *basso continuo* are required for both versions. The *basso continuo* partbook is labeled "Violon" on the title page and "Organo" where the music begins. It thus explicitly calls for performance on a low string instrument as well as for realization on the organ. In both Magnificats of this collection the text following the chant intonation is composed in its entirety.

### 1641, No. 17, Magnificat Primi Toni

Two four-part choirs (the second one of a somewhat lower tessitura than the first), two obligato treble instruments, and *basso continuo* are called for in this work. The choral writing is syllabic throughout the setting. Canticle Tone 1 supplies the intonation and cadence structure.

In this concise setting, the composer restricted himself to two basic textures. The first, as in the beginning verse on "anima mea Dominum," coordinates the two choirs rhythmically in an appropriate declamation of the text. As used in this texture, the second chorus does not merely duplicate the first chorus for volume; rather, it enriches the sonority of the tutti sections by strengthening triadic roots and fifths, while the thirds are handled with economy. The second basic texture combines one or several parts from the first chorus with a *basso continuo*, in most cases without participation of the treble instruments. The vocal writing in these passages usually departs from synchronized declamation and is characterized instead by either single or paired imitative entries.

However, unlike the through-composed Magnificat from the 1614 collection (No. 8), the alternate employment of these two styles is not governed here entirely by the traditional division into even- and odd-numbered verses. In this *Magnificat Primi Toni*, each verse has its individual pattern. Some of the verses (nos. 2, 5, 7, 9, and 11) are set throughout for small ensemble. Polychoral treatment is especially interesting in the "Esurientes," because this verse shows most clearly how the second chorus adds a completely new musical dimension to an intrinsically self-sufficient setting. In the "Deposuit" the obligato instruments are treated in a true concertizing manner to complement the solo bass. For the tutti sections, the instruments simply add to the color and sharpen the articulation of the declamatory rhythm.

## Performance Practice

For performance of this music, its original liturgical purpose must be kept in mind. Vesper services, even as celebrated in many Protestant churches, are the most appropriate occasions. A choir of three voices to a part is quite sufficient.

This music was written exclusively for male voices. Therefore, when the Magnificat settings are sung by a choir of mixed voices, women altos, in particular, must aim for a clear, well-defined sound, rather than for a big, rich tone. The proper musical expressiveness will be found if each phrase of the text in its proper inflection is set forth with dignified simplicity. Nineteenth-century dynamics are completely out of place.

For the works without specific *continuo* parts, discreet doubling of the voices on the organ does not violate the style. For performance of the organ parts in the settings from the 1614 and 1641 collections see Barnes-Ostrander, Appendix, p. xv. Because most present-day churches do not have two organs, the two different *basso continuo* parts provided for these three works had best be realized by one organist, with a low melody instrument doubling the lowest line of the music.

For those Magnificats where Stadlmayr made a polyphonic setting for only the even-numbered verses, the performance should be completed by singing the odd-numbered verses to the appropriate plain-chant formula for each work; these formulae are indicated in the discussion of the individual works, above. The text of the odd-numbered Magnificat verses is as follows:

1. Magnificat
   anima mea Dominum.

3. Quia respexit humilitatem ancillae suae
   ecce enim ex hoc beatam me dicent omnes generationes.

5. Et misericordia eius a progenie in progenies
   timentibus eum.

7. Deposuit potentes de sede,
   et exaltavit humiles.

9. Suscepit Israel puerum suum,
   recordatus misericordiae suae.

11. Gloria Patri, et Filio,
    et Spiritui Sancto.

## The Edition

This edition contains eight Magnificat settings by Stadlmayr taken from four seventeenth-century prints; the settings are entitled *Magnificat super Spuntavan già*, 1603, No. 1; *Magnificat super D'un si bel fuoco*, 1603, No. 3; *Magnificat*, 1603, No. 7; *Magnificat [Quarti Toni]*, 1603, No. 9; *Magnificat Primi Toni*, 1608, No. 1; *Magnificat Laudans exultans*, 1614, No. 3; *Magnificat super Primum Tonum*, 1614, No. 8; and *Magnificat Primi Toni*, 1641, No. 17. Although manuscript concordances exist for some of these prints (e.g., the publications of 1603 and 1608), the editor has chosen the prints as primary sources in each case because dedications and prefaces indicate that these publications

were probably issued with the approval of the composer.[25] Transcriptions were made of Magnificat settings that demonstrate various aspects of Stadlmayr's art and style; however, as mentioned above, none of the eight extant settings for more than eight voices (there is one *à* 10, and seven *à* 12) has been included here. Thus the compositions in this edition can be performed by the relatively small groups found in some churches and around college music departments.

The primary sources, cited in the discussion of the individual Magnificat compositions, did not present any unusual problems in the preparation of the present edition. Standard modern practice was followed regarding the indication of the original incipits, the editorial use of barlines, and the spelling, syllabification, and punctuation of the Magnificat text. Where the repetition of a text phrase was indicated in the source by "*ij*," this edition simply repeats that text without comment; the syllabic nature of the music leaves no doubt concerning the correct text underlay.

The partbook sources are consistent in their labeling of the first four vocal parts as Discantus, Altus, Tenor, and Bassus. However, there is no consistency in assigning labels to additional parts, such as Quinta Vox, Sexta Vox, etc. The placement of these parts in this full-score edition was determined by their range and tessitura, as is the modern custom.

In all of the present works except for 1603, No. 7, and 1614, No. 8, the note values in the original prints, largely minims and semi-minims, conform to the notation of their secular models. Because these note values proved practical for modern performance, they were not changed for the edition. However, note values were halved for the two works where the original notation, reflecting the common seventeenth-century practice for sacred music, was largely in semibreves and minims. Ligatures in the sources are designated here by overhead continuous brackets ( ⌐‾‾‾¬ ), and passages in coloration are indicated by broken brackets ( ⌐   ¬ ). The use of ligatures and coloration in the source publications appears to be a purely notational carry-over from an earlier age; the musical intent is clear without them.

Editorial accidentals, in square brackets, adapt the original notation to present-day convention; accidentals in parentheses function merely to caution retention of certain accidentals, as for instance, where cross-relations occur.

## Critical Notes

*1603, No. 1, Magnificat super Spuntavan già*

Verse 2

M. 18, Bassus, note 2 printed erroneously, upside down and on d.

Verse 6

Mm. 39-40, Altus, text underlay is "mente cordis

sui" here, which does not fit the musical accent; corrected to "dispersit superbos" by analogy with Discantus and Quinta Vox.

### Verse 10

M. 4, Discantus, note 4 is an eighth-note. Mm. 11, note 5 - m. 18, Altus part has a tenor clef (C4) instead of the correct mezzo-soprano clef (C2).

### 1603, No. 3, Magnificat super D'un si bel fuoco

### Verse 12

M. 12, Altus, note 1 is a quarter-note.

### 1603, No. 7, Magnificat

In each verse, the Altus part is marked with an S-like sign where the second voice of the canon (the *comes*) enters in the Septima Vox. The same sign marks the end of the canon in the Altus of each verse while the strict imitation in the Septima Vox is being carried to the end.

### Verse 2

Mm. 1-9, Sexta Vox has a mezzo-soprano clef (C2) instead of the correct tenor clef (C4). M. 9, Sexta Vox, note 2 is a quarter-note.

### Verse 4

M. 7, Septima Vox, rest 1 is a semibreve-rest (= half-rest), corrected here to a quarter-rest by analogy with Altus, m. 5.

### Verse 8

M. 6, Tenor, note 3 is b-flat.

### Verse 12

M. 24, Bassus, notes 1 and 2 are blotted out, except for partial stems that indicate the logical choice of pitches as d, d.

### 1614, No. 3, Magnificat Laudans exultans

### Verse 4

The triple meter is indicated in the Cantus I as O $\frac{3}{2}$ and in all other parts as $\phi \frac{3}{2}$.

### 1614, No. 8, Magnificat super Primum Tonum

### Verse 2

M. 18, Bassus II, note 1 is B-natural.

### 1641, No. 17, Magnificat Primi Toni

M. 52, Cantus I, note 4, the flat belonging to the B is placed before the d''. M. 67, Violin I, note 3 is f''-sharp; Cantus I, Altus II, Bassus I, and Bassus II, note 1, there is a conflict among these parts, and thus within each chorus, as to whether this note is g-natural or g-sharp—Cantus I and Bassus II have g-sharp, while Altus II and Bassus I have g-natural; the present editor suggests the g-sharp.

## Acknowledgments

A number of scholars and librarians have provided generous assistance at various stages of the studies leading to this publication. Among them I am especially indebted to Olga Buth, Gernot Gruber, Altman Kellner, Alexander Hyatt King, Herbert Livingston, Carol MacClintock, August Scharnagl, and Walter Senn.

For providing information, permitting direct access to sources, and making microfilms available, grateful acknowledgments are made to the following institutions: The British Museum (Magnificat publication of 1603); Proskesche Musikbibliothek, Regensburg (Magnificat publication of 1608, S.A.B. only); Bayerische Staatsbibliothek, Munich (Mus. Mss. 88, containing all parts of the pieces in the 1608 publication); the Music Library of The Ohio State University (Stadlmayr publication of 1614 and Stadlmayr publication of 1641 contained in the microfilm collection of the Deutsches Musikgeschichtliches Archiv, Kassel).

Most of all I want to thank my collaborator Marilyn Barnes-Ostrander for her invaluable contribution in dealing with the theoretical and the practical aspects of the keyboard realizations.

Hilde Junkermann
July 1980
Milwaukee, Wisconsin

# Notes

1. See also Hilde H. Junkermann, "The Magnificats of Johann Stadlmayr," (Ph.D. diss., The Ohio State University, 1967; University Microfilms, No. 67-6330); Walter Senn, "Stadlmayr," *Die Musik in Geschichte und Gegenwart*, ed. Friedrich Blume (Kassel, 1965), 12: cols. 1127-1153.

2. *Missae 8 v. cum duplici basso ad organum* (Augsburg: J. Krueger, 1596); no known copy; cited [incorrectly as 1569] by G. Draudius in *Bibliotheca classica*, 2d ed. (Frankfurt, 1625), p. 1636. A publication of 1610 with the same title is probably a later edition of these Masses.

3. *Sacrum Beatissimae Virginis Mariae Canticum 5.6.7.8.v.* (Munich, 1603). The first four Magnificat settings in the present edition are taken from this publication.

4. See Michael Praetorius, *Syntagma musicum*, vol. III, *Termini musici* (Wolfenbüttel, 1619; facsimile reprint, Kassel, 1958), p. 243. Wolfgang Caspar Printz, *Historische Beschreibung der Edelen Sing- und Klingkunst* (Dresden, 1690), p. 134.

5. Johann Stadlmayr, *Hymnen*, ed. J.E. Habert, in *Denkmäler der Tonkunst in Österreich*, III/1, Vol. V (1896; reprint, Graz, 1959). Habert's edition contains only the first volume, simple four-part settings based on plainsong tunes, of the original publication *Hymni quibus totius anni...* (Innsbruck, 1628).

6. The *Cantici Mariani septies variati liber quartus, vocum duodecim, cum triplici basso ad organum accomodato* was dedicated to Archduke Maximilian, who was to die later that same year.

7. Stadlmayr's *Psalmi vespertini omnes cum II Magnificat concertationibus musicis per VI voces et basso continuo* was dedicated to Abbott Andreas of Wilten (near Innsbruck). The second collection, *Psalmi integri a quatuor vocibus concertantibus quatuor accessorijs ad libitum accinendis cum 2 cornet: sive Violin*, was dedicated to Archduke Karl Ferdinand and his mother, Archduchess Claudia.

8. See, for instance, Joachim Burmeister, *Musica poetica* (Rostock, 1606), facsimile reprint in *Documenta musicologica*, ed. Martin Ruhnke (Kassel, 1955), I: no. X. Carl Dahlhaus, "Musica poetica und musikalische Poesie," *Archiv für Musikwissenschaft* XXIII/2 (July 1966): 110-124; the footnotes contain extensive bibliographic information.

9. See *Liber Usualis* (Desclee: New York, 1961), pp. 207-218, for these Canticle formulae and their relationship to the ecclesiastical modes. See also Gustave Reese, "The Polyphonic Magnificat of the Renaissance as a Design in Tonal Centers," *Journal of the American Musicological Society* XIII (1960): 68-78.

10. See *Liber Usualis*, pp. 207-218.

11. Luca Marenzio, *Il primo libro de madrigali a cinque voci* (Venice, 1580), No. 3.

12. The very extensive, controversial literature on the *chiavette* tends to convince one that attempts to find just one interpretation to fit all cases are ill-advised. See Junkermann, "The Magnificats of Johann Stadlmayr," pp. 37-39.

13. This is one of eight madrigals that were never published in any of Wert's own collections. *D'un si bel fuoco* appeared in the anthology *Musica di XIII autori illustri a cinque voci...* (Venice, 1576); see RISM: *Recueils imprimés XVIᵉ - XVIIᵉ siècles*, ed. F. Lesure (Munich, 1960), No. 1576/5.

14. Kremsmünster, Stiftsbibliothek, Chorbuch *L1*. See Fr. Altman Kellner, *Musikgeschichte des Stiftes Kremsmünster* (Kassel, 1956), pp. 157-158. According to a letter received from Father Kellner in October 1962, there is good reason to believe that this undated choirbook was compiled sometime during the years 1589 and 1590. See Junkermann, "The Magnificats of Johann Stadlmayr," p. 5.

15. *Antiphonale monasticum pro diurnis horis*, ed. Benedictines of Solesmes (Paris, 1934).

16. Published by Nenninger in Passau.

17. These are in the Proske Library in Regensburg.

18. According to Father Kellner's letter of 15 October 1962, *L5* has the same watermark and was written by the same hand as *L1*. Another undated choirbook containing all eight of these Magnificat settings is part of the Stellfeld collection, acquired in 1954 by the University of Michigan in Ann Arbor.

19. We do not know what special significance this dedication to the Öttingen Madonna had in Stadlmayr's life.

20. See footnote 9.

21. Otto Kinkeldey found this organ score among the earliest of its kind to be published in a German-speaking land. See his *Orgel und Klavier in der Musik des 16. Jahrhunderts* (Leipzig, 1910), p. 213.

22. RISM 1613/2. It is not clear if the discrepancy in the titles ("Laudans exultans," as opposed to "Laudans exultet") is due to careless copying or to Stadlmayr's use of another copy of this model, where the title may have differed from the one in the Schadeus anthology.

23. None of the usual reasons for such notation (requiring transposition) seem to apply—situations sometimes connected with the use of *chiavette* include adaptation to the tuning of a specific organ and accommodation of exceptionally high ranges in the voice parts. See Praetorius, *Syntagma musicum*, III: 80-81. Perhaps this is additional evidence that Stadlmayr, who followed his model so closely in other ways, knew the Croce motet through a different copy.

24. Praetorius, *Syntagma musicum*, III: 51. For a recent survey of the extensive literature on the subject, see Wolf Frobenius, "Tactus," in *Handwörterbuch der musikalischen Terminologie*, ed. H. H. Eggebrecht (Wiesbaden, 1971). In historical perspective, these inconsistencies appear to be symptoms of the gradual change from a mensural system to one concerned with tempo indications.

25. See Junkermann, "The Magnificats of Johann Stadlmayr," pp. 4-5, for a listing of the concordances.

# Appendix

## COMMENTARY ON THE
## BASSO CONTINUO REALIZATIONS

That Johann Stadlmayr should have, in 1614, written pieces employing a thoroughbass is not in itself remarkable. He was simply demonstrating his knowledge of the *stile nuovo*, a style that was to be greatly appreciated by his future patron, Leopold V. What is more worthy of commentary is the composer's prescription for not one but two *continuo* parts in two of the Magnificats of the present collection.[1] (Of the eight Magnificat settings in this edition, three have *continuo* accompaniment. These three are 1614, No. 3; 1614, No. 8; and 1641, No. 17.) Yet even this apparent innovativeness is somewhat deceptive, as is made clear by examining the actual function of the *basso continuo* lines. These lines adhere closely to the choral bass parts (or to whatever tone is lowest) in the manner of the old *basso seguente*.[2]

The thoroughbass accompaniment in the choral sections is thus rendered texturally superfluous. Possibly, Stadlmayr was more interested in the sonoral weight that could be lent by the organ or other *continuo* instruments than in the harmonic and textural support of a later style of *continuo* accompaniment.

This observation of the dual capacity of the *continuo* accompaniment (i.e., the *continuo* could lend both sonoral weight and harmonic and textural support) leads directly to one of the problems of performing the works in this volume, the choice of *continuo* instrument(s). The organ was, of course, the established vehicle for the accompaniment of church music; however, evidence that Stadlmayr himself used two organs is purely circumstantial. Indeed, it is not necessary to assume that the *continuo* accompaniment was limited to organ alone (see below). The impressive inventory of instruments owned by the Archduke at Innsbruck in 1596 included the following, reserved for use in the chapel: 37 violas or viols, 27 trumpets, 20 trombones, 23 zinks, 35 "pipes," 12 flutes, and 12 shawms, as well as lute, crumhorn, and bassoon; while among those instruments used by the amateurs at court were organs, keyboard instruments, harps, lutes, and dulcimer. A special showpiece of the castle was an enclosed "house organ." A one-manual organ (signed with the date 1614) was added to the Silver Chapel later.[3] In addition to the chapel organ, other organs may have been available for performance.

Thus, while it is quite possible that a choir organ or a small cabinet organ was used to play the second *continuo* part, it is also possible that this second part was played by other instruments. There were early-seventeenth-century precedents for *continuo* performance on instruments other than the organ. For example, the frontispiece of Monteverdi's *Vespro della Beata Vergine* of 1610 lists two flutes, two recorders, three cornetti, three trombones, violins, *viole* and *celli di repieno, organo principale, organo di coro*, cembalo, and, as *bassus generalis*, either bassoon and contrabassoon or violoncello, viola da gamba, and contrabass.[4] Similarly, Banchieri reported hearing a composition with an elaborate *continuo* group consisting of "deu violoni continoi in contrabasso, due clavecembali, tre liuti, due chitarroni," in addition to the organ.[5] In his *St. John Passion* of 1643, T. Selle followed the same precedent, using the organ to accompany the chorus, and the regal for solo sections.[6] The title page for the voice parts of the first and second choirs in Schütz's *Polychoral Psalms* (1619) suggests "Orgel/Lauten/Chitaron/ etc." as accompaniment instruments; and his *Ascension Story* and *Christmas Story* call for such instruments as positif organ, harpsichord, pandora or lute, as well as viola da gamba or violone.[7]

Since many of the aforementioned instruments may not be available for modern performance, the realizations in the present edition were made with the organ in mind. However, any performance plans should not overlook the fact that Stadlmayr's contemporaries admitted multiple instrumental possibilities for the performance of works of this sort.

The same flexible attitude should be adopted with respect to the ornamentation within these realizations. While numerous writers of early- and mid-seventeenth-century books of instruction concerning the figured bass[8] cautioned the accompanist against excessive ornamentation and the adding of dissonances, examples given in these treatises and vocal scores of the period clearly indicate that some simple and tasteful ornamentation was generally added to what would otherwise have been block chords. Aichinger, Viadana, and Schütz[9] all recommended that the organist provide himself with a guide by writing out his part in full. Such a practice would have enabled the organist to supply not only appropriate ornamentation, but also occasional contrapuntal material to fill in the texture.

Guidance for organ registration is provided by notes left in early-seventeenth-century Austrian organs. An example of the type of instrument Stadlmayr might have had at his disposal is the organ in the Benedictine Abbey of Weingarten, which was built in 1558 with the following stops:[10]

| Hauptwerk | Positiv | Pedal |
|---|---|---|
| Praestant | Praestant | Praestant |
| Gross Hohlflöte | Hohlflöte | Oktave |
| Quintadena | Oktave | Superoktave |
| Oktave | Schwegel | Mixtur |
| Klein Hohlflöte | Hörnli | Posaune |
| Superoktave | Vogelgesang | Tremulant |
| Schwegel | | |
| Mixtur | | |
| Zimbel | | |
| Rauschwerk | | |

This scheme was typical of the organs at Innsbruck and other cities in southern Germany.

The two examples of seventeenth-century organ registration cited below demonstrate the kinds of stops typically used to accompany a work for chorus and soloists. Accompaniments for solo episodes tended to use only one or two stops and were quite distinct from those for tutti passages. A Berlin manuscript of Schütz's *Psalm 150* interspersed the following handwritten reminders to the organist for registration changes to serve the changing textual imagery and musical style within the psalm:[11]

Tutti
Quintadena
Tutti
Dulcian Rückpositiv
Tutti
Grobgedackt
Posaunen
Rückpositiv Kleingedackt
Tutti
Grobgedackt im Oberwerk
Rückpositiv Spitz[flöte]
Oberwerk Rückpositiv Grosses Werck klein +
Rückpositiv grobgedackt
Cymbel
Tutti
Rückpositiv
Tutti

Monteverdi himself marked instructions to the organist in his *Magnificat I* for seven voices and six instruments (1610). In this case the registration was to be changed for each of the twelve verses of the canticle as follows:[12] (1) Principale solo, principale e ottava, principale ottava e quintadecima; (2) Soprano solo canta; principale solo; (3) Principale ottava et quintadecima; (4) Principale solo; (5) Principale solo et suona adaggio perchè le parti cantano e suonano in croma et semicroma; (6) Principale solo; (7) Principale et registro delle zifare e voci humane; (8) Principale solo; cornetti responde à quel di sopra in Echo; (9) Principale e ottava; (10) Principale solo, si suona adaggio perchè il duoi soprani cantano di echo; (11) Principale solo; (12) Principale solo; [then] organo pieno.

Final decisions concerning registration in performance of the Stadlmayr Magnificats must, of course, be made according to the sound of the instrument to be used, the size of the chorus, and the characteristics of the hall. Choices should be consistent with the practice of Stadlmayr's time, in which the fundamental *continuo* stop to accompany a single voice was an 8' stopped diapason, for choral sections an 8' principal plus 16' and 8' on the pedals, and possibly a soft reed to give emphasis to the bass line.[13] The additional stops given in the two preceding lists suggest other appropriate choices to the organist.

Like his contemporaries, Stadlmayr used figures sparingly in the Magnificats 1614, No. 3; 1614, No. 8; and 1641, No. 17. Indeed, the *continuo* line is largely unfigured, except for those few instances where the desired chord or ornament was somewhat unusual.

The chief problems in realizing Stadlmayr's *continuo* lines in these Magnificats stems from the fact that while their *continuo* parts were intended mainly for accompanying choruses rather than soloists, the guides to *continuo* realization left to us by seventeenth-century writers of thoroughbass manuals concern themselves largely with elementary explanations of the figures and with certain technical details that are really relevant only to the accompaniment of soloists.[14] In general, the various treatises consulted dealt with one of two fundamental styles of accompaniment. One style furnishes a simple, essentially chordal background; the other supplies a more linear element to the *continuo* texture, as though it were an instrumental proxy for absent vocal lines. This latter effect was expressly intended for such sacred concerti as those by Viadana and Aichinger, and it was generally regarded as the more appropriate model for realizing the *continuo* part in a church motet; a more vertical texture was considered suitable for secular monody.[15] In the choral sections of the Magnificats in the present edition, the realizations generally duplicate the vocal parts, with little embellishment.[16] The accompaniment in solo sections aims to support their more elaborate style with corresponding ornamentation.

Certain other technical problems should also be mentioned here. Seventeenth-century authorities generally agree that *bassetti* (i.e., passages in the *continuo* part that incorporate one of the upper vocal parts when the actual bass voice has dropped out) are to be played only on the manuals. Fugal entries are to be played first with one voice alone. Both Praetorius and

Viadana imply that the accompaniment may become free upon the entrance of other voices, whereas Poglietti strictly enjoins the performer to play only with one additional finger, or line, as each successive fugal voice enters.

The distinction between the styles of the choral sections on the one hand, and the more florid solo sections on the other, seemed to require a similar distinction between the types of ornaments used in each style. The ubiquitous cadential suspension and the varied texture and rhythm of parts may be seen in the best examples of the period, such as those by Agazzari and Praetorius. Passing tones, accelerating trills, appoggiaturas, and slides were among the most typical embellishments of the early seventeenth century, as shown both by contemporary authorities and by the musical compositions of the era.[17]

No single exclusive solution to problems of performance of any *continuo* part can be offered. These realizations are a guide to the performer, who should interpret his or her part with the same care—and freedom—as his or her baroque counterpart.

July 1980

Marilyn Barnes-Ostrander
Troy, New York

# Notes to the Appendix

1. There were some earlier examples of sacred compositions for two choruses and two *continuo* parts; for example, Girolamo Dorati's *Nisi Dominus*, from the collection with the title page that reads "Hieronymi Doratii *Lucensis Psalmi ad Vesperas pro totius anni solemnitatibus Duoq. Cantica B. Virginis, omnia octonis vocibus concinenda, Addita partium gravium divisione pro Organi pulsatoris commoditate, nunc primum in lucem editi* (Venetijs: Apud Iacobum Vincentium, 1609)." This work is transcribed in Jeffrey Gordon Kurtzman, "The Monteverdi Vespers of 1610 and Their Relationship with Italian Sacred Music of the Early Seventeenth Century" (Ph.D. diss., University of Illinois, 1972), II: 574-588; this dissertation also reprints two other works written for two choruses and two organ parts: Giov. Francesco Capello, *Dominus Deus Israel* (Verona, 1612); and Giovanni Ghizzolo, *Magnificat* (Milan, 1613).

2. In this respect Stadlmayr is no different from his contemporaries who were working in the same medium. Cf. the numerous works transcribed by Kurtzman, "The Monteverdi Vespers," II. See also Paul Winter, *Der Mehrchörige Stil; historische Hinweise fur die heutige Praxis* (Frankfurt, London, New York: C. F. Peters, 1964), pp. 68 ff.; Helmut Haack, *Anfange des Generalbass-Satzes; die "Cento concerti ecclesiastici" (1602) von Lodovico Viadana* (Tutzing: Verlegt bei Hans Schneider, 1974), vol. II; and Gregor Aichinger, *Cantiones ecclesiasticae*, ed. William E. Hettrick, Recent Researches in the Music of the Baroque Era, vol. XIII (Madison: A-R Editions, 1972).

3. *Die Musik in Geschichte und Gegenwart* (1957), s.v. "Innsbruck," by Walter Senn.

4. Claudio Monteverdi, *Vespro della Beata Vergine* (1610), ed. Walter Goehr (Vienna: Universal Edition, 1956), p. ix, reproduces the frontispiece in facsimile.

5. A. Banchieri, *Conclusioni nel suono dell'organo* (Bologna, 1609), pp. 50-51; cited in Peter Williams, "Basso Continuo on the Organ," *Music and Letters* L (1969): 136-152, 230-245. Williams cites several examples of the use of *continuo* instruments other than or in addition to the organ in the performance of devotional or church music.

6. Peter Williams, *Figured Bass Accompaniment* (Edinburgh: At the University Press, 1970), I: 26.

7. Gerhard Kirchner, *Der Generalbass bei Heinrich Schütz* (Kassel, New York: Bärenreiter, 1960), pp. 23-25.

8. In addition to the sources already cited, the most important treatises that provided the background for these realizations were: Agostino Agazzari, *Del Sonare sopra'l basso con tutti li stromenti e dell'uso loro nel conserto* (Siena, 1607; facs. ed., Bibliotheca Musica Bononiensis, Bologna: Forni Editore, 1969); Heinrich Albert, Preface to *Anderer Theil der Arien* (Königsberg, 1640), reprinted in *Denkmäler der deutscher Tonkunst*, ed. Eduard Bernoulli (Leipzig: Breitkopf & Härtel, 1903), Set. I, Vol. 12; Wolfgang Ebner, Rules published in Herbst's *Arte Prattica et poetica* (Frankfurt, 1653), quoted and translated in F. T. Arnold, *The Art of Accompaniment from a Thoroughbass* (London: The Holland Press, 1961), I: 131 ff.; Georg Muffat, *An Essay on Thoroughbass*, ed. Hellmut Federhofer (Tübingen: American Institute of Musicology, 1961); Alessandro Poglietti, *Compendium oder Kurtzer Begriff und Einführung zur Musica* (MS, 1676), quoted extensively in Federhofer's preface to his edition of Muffat's *Essay on Thoroughbass*; Johann Jacob Prinner, *Musicalischer Schlissl* (MS, 1677), quoted extensively by Federhofer in his edition of Muffat's *Essay*; Michael Praetorius, *Syntagma musicum* (Wittenberg, 1619; facs. ed. by Willibald Gurlitt, Kassel: Bärenreiter, 1958), Vol. III; Diego Ortiz, *Tratado de glosas sobre clausulas y otros generos de puntos en la musica de puntos en la musica de violones* (Roma, 1553), translated into German by Max Schneider (Kassel: Bärenreiter, 1967); Lorenzo Penna da Bologna, *Li Primi Albori musicali, per li principianti della Musica figurata* (Bologna: Giacomo Monti, 1679); Heinrich Schütz, Preface to *Psalmen Davids* (1619), in *Neue Ausgabe sämtlicher Werke*, ed. Wilhelm Ehmann (Kassel, Basel: Bärenreiter, 1971), Vol. 23, pp. xii-xx.

9. Aichinger, *Cantiones ecclesiasticae*, pp. viii-ix. Viadana, Rule 6, quoted by Haack, *Anfange*, p. xv. Heinrich Schütz, Preface to *Cantiones Sacrae* (1625), *Neue Ausgabe sämtlicher Werke*, ed. Gottfried Grote (Kassel, Basel: Bärenreiter, 1960), Vol. 8: xvii, xxiv-xxvi.

10. Peter Williams, *The European Organ, 1450-1850* (London: B.T. Batsford, Ltd., 1968), p. 65.

11. Kirchner, *Der Generalbass*, p. 31. These instructions corresponded to sections of the *Psalm 150*, differentiated from each other by means of either medium (chorus or solo) or text. Solo sections used single stops for accompaniment in this list. The cymbal and trombone were used when the text referred to these instruments. The tenth and eleventh items in the list, "Grobgedackt im Oberwerk" and "Rückpositiv Spitz" occurred within the same section, i.e., "Lobet ihn mit Pauken." The + sign probably meant to couple the three manuals (or subdivisions of the organ).

The manuscript also contained a second list of organistic annotations, in a different color ink, which, though less instructive because it used a set of numbers rather than names of stops, did show that solo sections might have accompaniments using as many as three stops. Both lists are combined in the citation given by Hans Joachim Moser, *Heinrich Schütz: His Life and Work*, trans. from 2nd rev. ed. by Carl F. Pfatteicher (St. Louis: Concordia Publishing House, 1959), p. 326.

12. Also printed in Monteverdi, *Vespro*.

13. Williams, "Basso Continuo," p. 150.

14. For example, Agazzari, *Del Sonare*, p. 8, admonished the organist not to play the same notes as those being sung by a soprano; Johann Staden, *Kurzer und einfältiger Bericht* (Nuremberg, 1626), trans. by Arnold, *The Art of Accompaniment*, p. 102, explained such oversights as the fact that the figures 4 3 sometimes mean 4 #; Poglietti, *Compendium*, quoted by Federhofer in Muffat, *Essay*, p. 9, explained that when the bass clef was used, the right hand should not go higher than d'' in the discant nor lower than f in the tenor.

15. This point is made by Williams, "Basso Continuo," pp. 139-140. See also Max Schneider, *Die Anfänge des Basso Continuo und seiner Bezifferung* (Leipzig: Breitkopf & Härtel, 1918; republished, Westmead, Farnborough, Hants, England: Gregg International Publishers, Ltd., 1971), pp. 16 ff.; and Hans Heinrich Eggebrecht, "Arten des Generalbasses im frühen und mittleren 17. Jahrhundert," *Archiv für Musikwissenschaft* XIV (1957): 61-82. But cf. Fritz Oberdoerffer, "Neuere Generalbaßstudien," *Acta Musicologica* XXXIX (1967): 182-201.

16. Some authorities are stricter than others. Penna, *Li Primi Albori*, Bk. III, ch. 14, endorses added embellishments in choral sections. Enrico Radesca, *Il quinto libro delle canzonette, madrigali et arie, a tre, a una, et a due voci* (Venice, 1617), cited by Robert Donington, *The Interpretation of Early Music* (new version; New York: St. Martin's Press, 1974), p. 180, pointed out that the use of embellishments would depend upon the performer's knowledge of counterpoint. Poglietti is quoted by Federhofer in Muffat, *Essay*, p. 11: "Dis ist die Manier, wie man die Fugen soll schlagen. *N.B.* so lang das Subjectum anfangs gehet, soll man mit ainem Finger allein schlagn, wan die ander[e] kombt, mit zweyen, die dritte mit dreyen." Viadana's preface is reprinted in Haack, *Anfange*; the rule in question is No. 5, pp. xiv-xv. Praetorius also allows a free accompaniment upon the entrance of the second voice in a fugue or imitative chorale. See his *Syntagma*, III: 138.

17. An excellent source for the kinds of embellishments that were typical of the period is Gio. Battista Bovicelli, *Regole, Passaggi di Mvsica* (Venice, 1594; facs., ed. Nanie Bridgman, Kassel, Basel: Bärenreiter-Verlag, 1957).

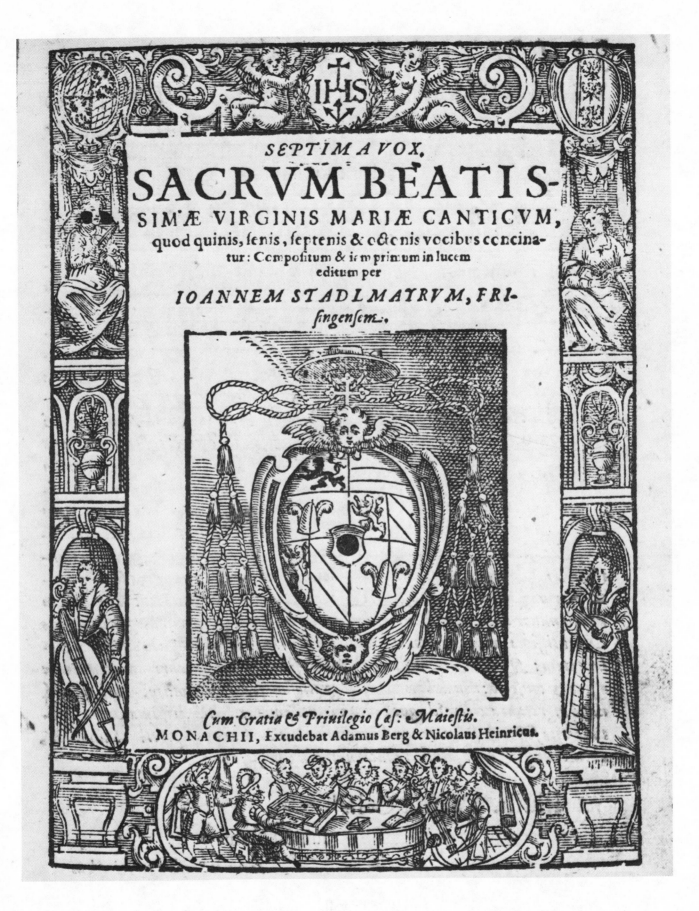

Plate I.
Johann Stadlmayr, *Sacrum Beatissimae Virginis Mariae Canticum* (1603), title page, Septima Vox partbook.
(Courtesy, Music Room, British Museum, London)

Plate II.
Johann Stadlmayr, *Sacrum Beatissimae Virginis Mariae Canticum* (1603), sample page of Septima Vox partbook
showing verses 2 and 4 of *Magnificat*, 1603, No. 7.
(Courtesy, Music Room, British Museum, London)

# SELECTED MAGNIFICATS

# Magnificat super Spuntavan già

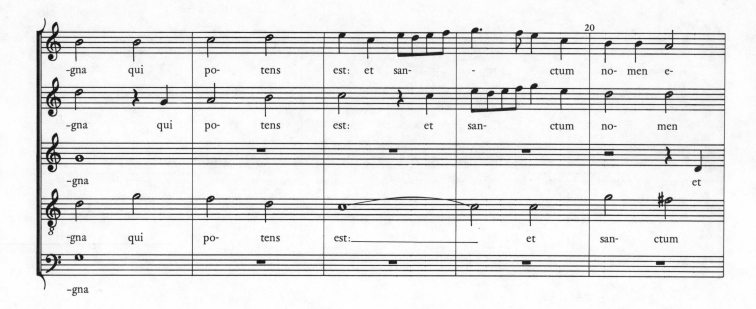

6

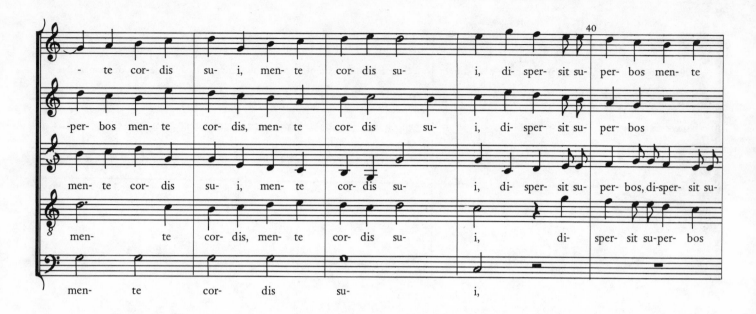

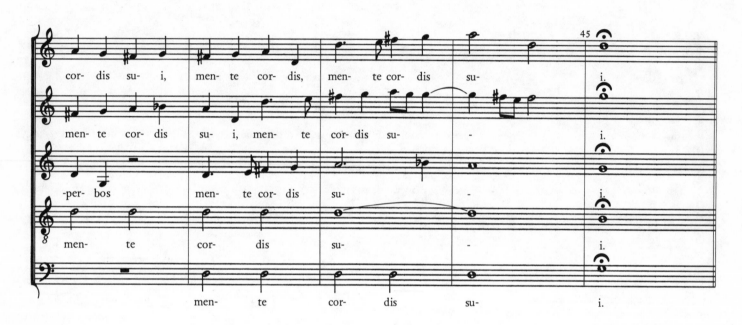

**8.**

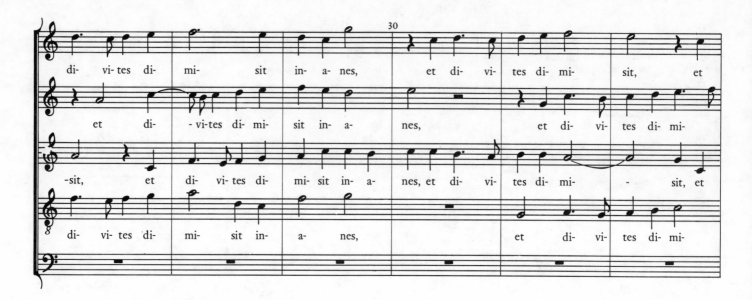

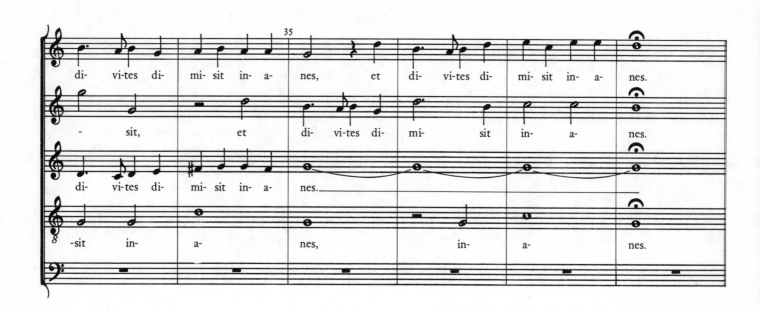

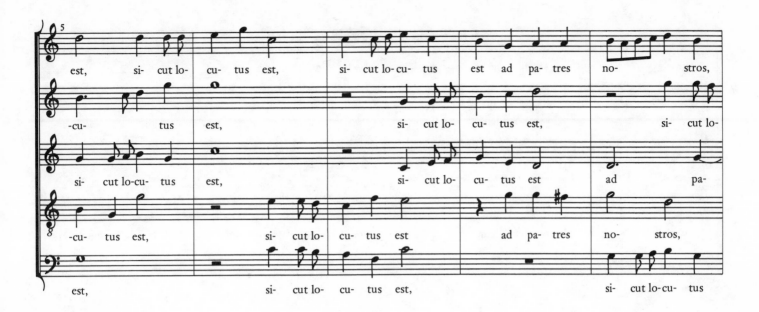

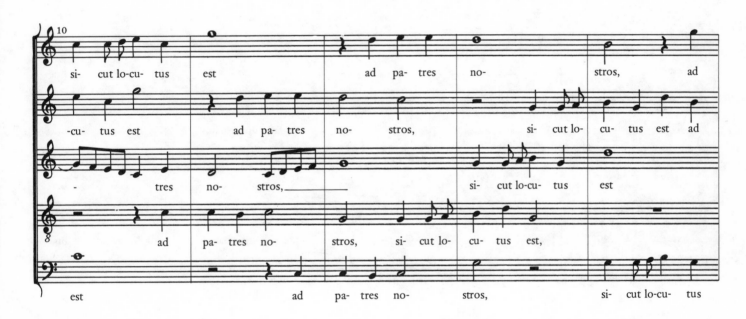

-stros, A- -bra- ham et se- mi- ni e- jus_____ in

A- -bra- ham et se- mi- ni e- jus in sae- cu-

-stros, A- -bra- ham et se- mi- ni e- -jus

-stros, A- -bra- ham et se- mi- ni e- -jus in

-stros,

sae- cu- la,_____ A- bra-

-la, in sae- cu- la, A- -bra- ham, A- bra-

in sae- -cu- la, A- bra- ham, A- bra-

sae- cu- la, A- -bra- ham, A- bra-

A- -bra- ham, A- bra-

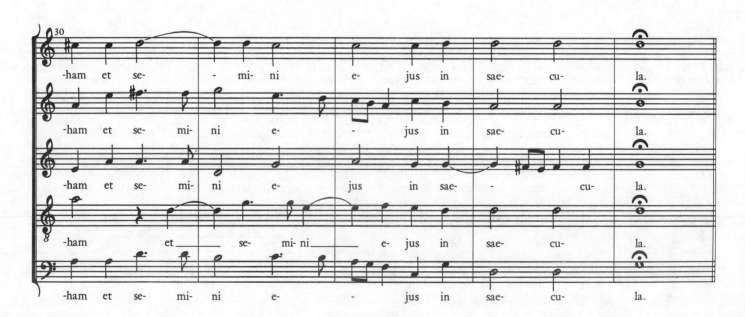

-ham et se- -mi- ni e- jus in sae- cu- la.

-ham et se- mi- ni e- -jus in sae- cu- la.

-ham et se- mi- ni e- jus in sae- -cu- la.

-ham et_____ se- mi- ni_____ e- jus in sae- cu- la.

-ham et se- mi- ni e- -jus in sae- cu- la.

**12.**

Si- cut e- rat, si- cut e-
Si- cut e- rat, si- cut e- rat, si- cut
Si- cut e- rat, si- cut e- rat, si- cut e-
Si- cut e- rat, si- cut e- rat, si- cut e- rat,
Si- cut e- rat, si- cut e- rat,

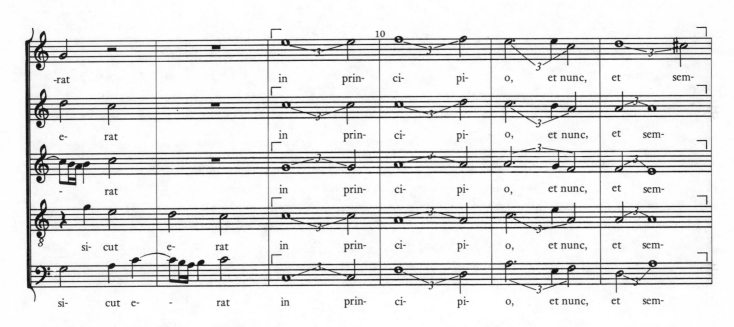

-rat in prin- ci- pi- o, et nunc, et sem-
e- rat in prin- ci- pi- o, et nunc, et sem-
-rat in prin- ci- pi- o, et nunc, et sem-
si- cut e- rat in prin- ci- pi- o, et nunc, et sem-
si- cut e- -rat in prin- ci- pi- o, et nunc, et sem-

-per, et in sae- -cu- la, et in sae- cu- la, et in
-per, et in sae- -cu- la, et in sae- cu- la, et in sae- cu-
-per, et in sae- cu- la, et in sae- cu- la, et in sae- cu- la, et in sae- cu-
-per, et in sae- cu- la, et in sae- cu- la, et in sae- cu- la,
-per, et in sae- cu- la, et in sae- cu- la sae- cu-

# Magnificat super D'un si bel fuoco

1603, No. 3

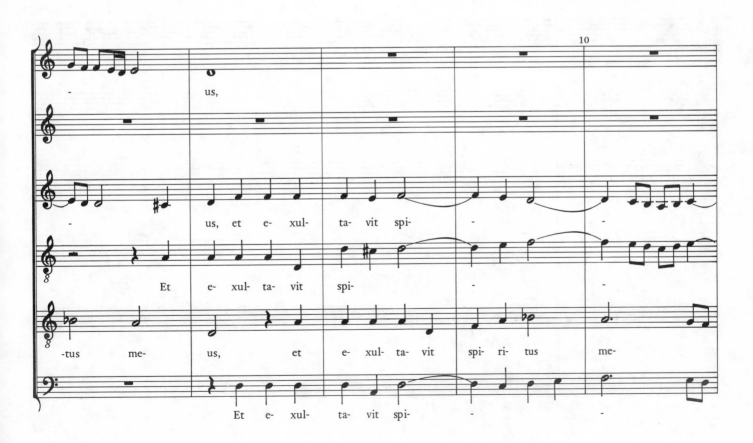

16

20

**6.**

Fe- cit po- ten- ti- am,                fe- cit____

Fe- cit po- ten- ti- am, fe- cit po- ten- ti- am,      fe-

Fe- cit po- ten- ti- am,                    fe- cit po-

Fe- cit po- ten- ti- am,                 fe-

Fe- cit po- ten- ti- am,

____ po- ten- ti- am, fe- cit____ po- ten- ti- am in bra- - chi-

Fe- cit____ po- ten- ti- am in bra-

-cit po- ten- ti- am, fe- cit____ po- ten- - ti- am in bra- - chi-

-ten- ti- am, fe- cit____ po- ten- ti- am in bra- - chi-

-cit po- ten- ti- am, fe- cit____ po- ten- - -

fe- cit____ po- ten- ti- am in____ bra-

26

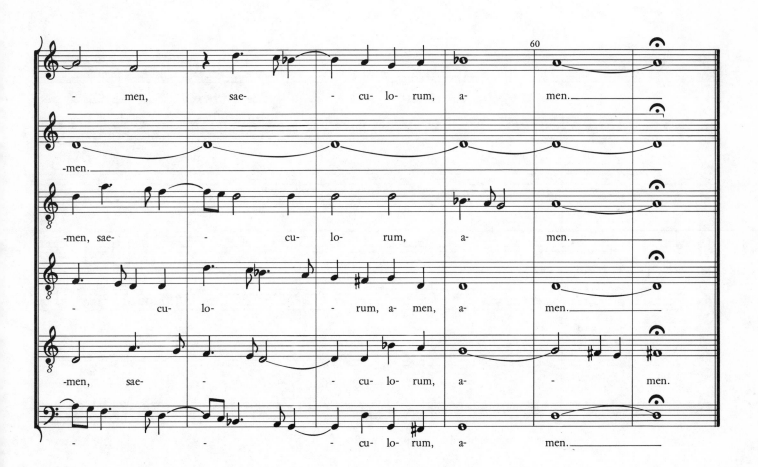

# Magnificat

1603, No.7

40

42

**8.**

48

**10.**

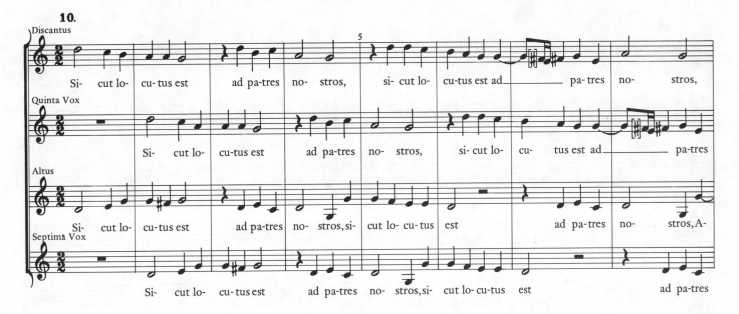

**12.**

# Magnificat Quarti Toni

1603, No.9

**8.**

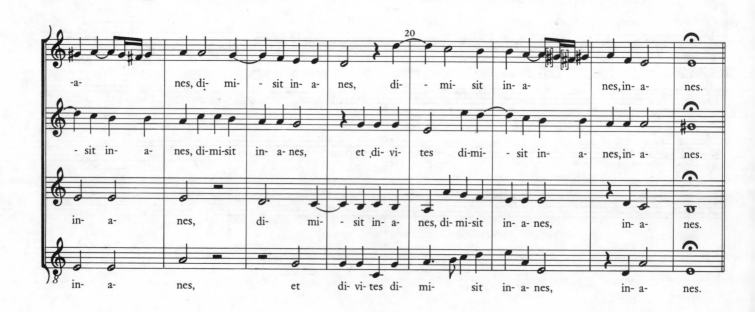

**10.**

64

**12.**

# Magnificat Primi Toni

1608, No.1

san-ctum no- men e- jus, et san- ctum no-men e - jus.

san- ctum no- men e- jus, et san- ctum no-men e- jus.

san- ctum no-men e - jus, et san-ctum no men e- jus.

et san- ctum no-men e - jus.

**6.**

Fe- cit po- ten- ti- am in bra- chi- o su- o: di- sper-

Fe- cit po- ten ti- am in bra-chi o su- o: di-sper- sit, di-

Fe- cit po- ten- ti- am in bra-chi o su- o: di-sper- sit, di-

Fe- cit po- ten- ti- am in bra-chi o su- o: di- sper-

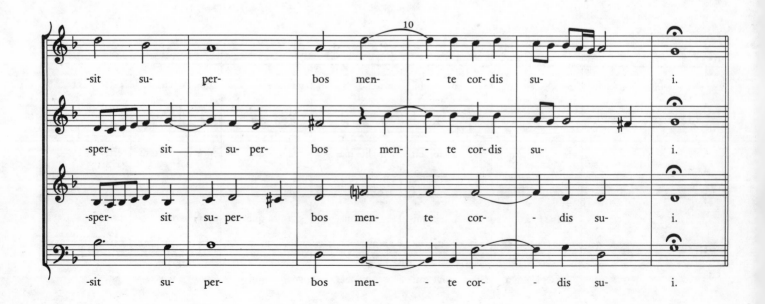

-sit su- per- bos men- te cor-dis su- i.

-sper- sit su- per- bos men- te cor-dis su- i.

-sper- sit su- per- bos men- te cor- dis su- i.

-sit su- per- bos men- te cor- dis su- i.

**8.**

E- su- ri- en- tes im- ple- vit bo- nis: et

E- su- ri- en- tes im- ple- vit bo- nis: et di-

E- su- ri- en- tes im- ple- vit bo- nis: et

E- su- ri- en- tes im- ple- vit bo- nis:

di- vi- tes di- mi- sit in- a- nes, di- mi- sit in- a-

-vi- tes di- mi- sit in- a- nes, et di- vi- tes di- mi- sit in- a-

di- vi- tes di- mi- sit in- a- nes,

et di- vi- tes di- mi- sit in- a-

-nes, et di- vi- tes di- mi- sit in- a- nes.

-nes, et di- vi- tes di- mi- sit in- a- nes.

et di- vi- tes di- mi- sit in- a- nes.

-nes, et di- vi- tes di- mi- sit in- a- nes.

**10.**

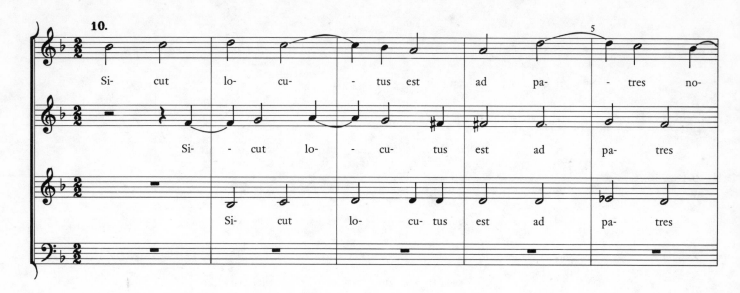

**12.**

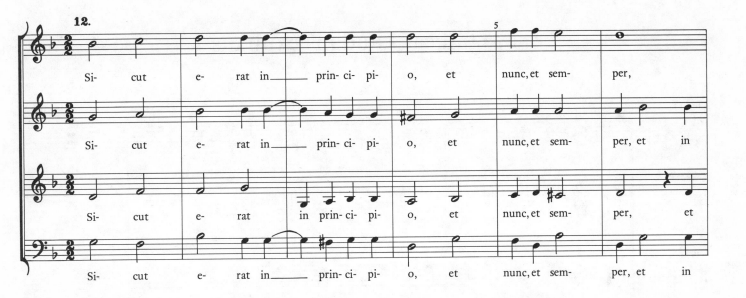

Si- cut e- rat in prin- ci- pi- o, et nunc, et sem- per,

Si- cut e- rat in prin- ci- pi- o, et nunc, et sem- per, et in

Si- cut e- rat in prin- ci- pi- o, et nunc, et sem- per, et

Si- cut e- rat in prin- ci- pi- o, et nunc, et sem- per, et in

et in sae- cu- la sae- cu-

sae- cu- la sae- cu- lo- rum, a- men, et in sae- cu- la sae- cu- lo-

in sae- cu- la sae- cu- lo- rum, a- men,

sae- cu- la sae- cu- lo- rum, a- men, et in sae- cu- la sae- cu-

-lo- rum, a- men, et in sae- cu- la sae- cu- lo- rum, a- men.

- rum, a- men, et in sae- cu- la sae- cu- lo- rum, a- men.

et in sae- cu- la sae- cu- lo- rum, a- men.

-lo- rum, a- men, sae- cu- lo- rum, a- men.

# Magnificat Laudans exultans

83

8.

E- su- ri- en- tes im- ple- vit

E- su- ri- en- tes im- ple- vit bo-

E- su- ri- en- tes im- ple- vit bo-

E- su- ri- en- tes im- ple- vit bo-

E- su- ri- en- tes im- ple- vit bo- nis,

E- su- ri- en- tes im- ple- vit bo- nis,

E- su- ri- en- tes im- ple- vit bo- nis,

E- su- ri- en- tes im- ple- vit bo- nis,

et di- vi- tes di- mi- sit in- a- nes.

et di- vi- tes di- mi- sit, di- mi- sit in- a- nes.

et_____ di- vi- tes di- mi- sit in- a- nes.

et di- vi- tes di- mi- sit in- a- nes.

-mi- sit, et_____ di- vi- tes di- mi- sit in- a- nes.

-tes di- mi- sit, et di- vi- tes di- mi- sit in- a- nes.

et di- vi- tes di- mi- sit, et di- vi- tes di- mi- - sit in- a- nes.

-tes di- mi- sit, et di- vi- tes di- mi- sit in- a- nes.

**10.**

100

# Magnificat super Primum Tonum

110

112

120

126

# Magnificat Primi Toni

1641, No.17

Et mi-se-ri-cor-di- a, mi-se-ri-cor-di-a e- jus a_____ pro-ge-ni- e in pro-ge-

Et mi-se-ri- cor-di- a, mi-se-ri- cor-di-a e- jus a pro- ge-ni- e in pro-

Et mi-se-ri- cor- di- a, mi-se-ri- cor-di- a e- jus a pro-ge- ni- e in pro-

Et mi-se-ri-cor-di- a, mi-se-ri-cor-di- a e- jus a_____ pro-ge-ni- e in pro-

5   6